# Puddles, Ponds and Piddles

(The Adventures of E. Toad A' Thomas and
His sister, T. Tiny Tadpole)

*Happy Reading!*
*Nancy Sharp*

# DEDICATION

Dedicated…to the memory of my Father. My earliest recollections are of him and his very funny, made-up bear stories. …to the memory of my Mother who filled my ears with wonderful, colorful stories. She put expression and imagination into my life. …to Johnny, my husband, for his constant encouragement by telling me to "write it down".

…to Skylar and Zane, two very bright lights in my life. They are happily living their own stories. …to Drake and Stephanie who lived the experiences of E. Toad and T. Tiny. Their lives are cherished memories.

"Life is not a series of isolated ponds and puddles; life is this river you see below, before you. It flows from the past through the present on its way to the future."

--I Know This Much Is True

Wally Lamb, page 610

# CONTENTS

# THE BIG CIRCLE

The sun was tossing rays in and out of the trees. Sometimes it looked like a speedy movie, sometimes a New Year's sparkler, but what E. Toad A' Thomas really liked about it was the polka dot effect it gave his stomach. He looked at himself, and a beautiful pattern flicked on and off. As he sat studying this design, he sailed on his big lily pad under a group of cattails, and the blinking left him. It was shady and cool. He pulled over to a big cattail and tied up his lily pad. He felt like being in a dark place. His eyes filled with tears. A great tear rolled down his face and into the water. He watched as the rippling circle it made got bigger and bigger and bigger and bigger. He wished the big circle could surround him and take him back home.

E. Toad loved his old house under the patio brick wall. But now they were in a new place, and it all seemed so different. "All toad families have to move sometime or other," said his mother. Daddy T. getting a better job was one good reason to move. But to have to relocate because a Kitty K. is making your life unpleasant just didn't seem right. Living under the patio brick wall had been great, but when the family (whose patio brick wall it really was) got a rather mean Kitty K., the toad family feared for their safety. That Kitty K. delighted in roughing up toads!  The family had grown many vegetables in their garden, and bugs had been so available for the A' Thomas family. Daddy T. said he ate so many bugs one night that he felt he had paid a year's rent.  It was moist and cool under that patio brick wall. This new place between the oak tree roots seemed so hot and dry.

So cool

But most of all E. Toad missed his friends.  He had not met a single kid toad.  Of course, he had moved his pet chameleon.  But Z. Chameleon Achoo had not found a friend either.  He missed playing hide and seek.  So they were both as lonesome as could be.  E. Toad saw some kid toads looking out of doors and windows as his family unpacked,

So HOT

but no one said "Hi", or "Come over" or "What's your name?"

He turned over on his stomach and buried his head under his arm. "How will I ever make it to school?" he thought. Walking into a strange room with all those big-eyed toads and frogs seemed scary! E. Toad moved his lily pad farther into the thickest cattails. He hoped in his heart that the sun wouldn't come up tomorrow and he wouldn't have to face that day. Or maybe, he thought, this is a dream. Maybe he really didn't move! Maybe I am by the bird feeder playing leap frog. Maybe, just maybe. He pinched himself real hard, and then he hollered . . . "Oh! Dear, it's for real. I did move."

The water stirred. Up came one big glassy yellow eye and then another.

"Whatever do you want? Don't you know you woke up my little sister with that yell? That hollow reed comes into the mud stack by our house, and I'm telling you, you gave us a scare."

"Oh! I didn't mean to. I got pinched. I am sorry," said E. Toad.

"Are you new in the neighborhood? We just got back from vacation, and I didn't know who had moved into the moss bed under the oak tree."

E. Toad
meets A. Froggy

"Yes, we moved in yesterday." E. Toad quickly flicked that tear from running down his cheek. "I really like it here. A lot better than where we were living. I've met a lot of new friends. I like the meadow and the pond."

"Well, my name is A. Froggy Franklin. We live on Reed Road right over there behind the mud stack. Hey, let's hook our lily pads and float together."

"I was kinda resting. But if you want to we can," answered E. Toad.

E. Toad wondered why his mouth was saying the words he heard. Why couldn't he just say he would love to because he's so lonesome and so sad and so unhappy? He didn't like himself at that minute. He felt even worse than he had earlier. But he found a leaf strip and quickly tied the lily pads together.

So lonesome
So Sad
So unhappy

"Here, you go first because you know the pond," said E. Toad. So they sat and sailed and talked. When they took a land break, they played hide and seek between the cattails and reeds. Then they had a dragonfly snack. All the time they laughed and talked and laughed. The aching left E. Toad's heart. He listened as A. Froggy told him about the school and the new store and the area around the pond. He told A. Froggy about the patio brick wall, and the garden and the bird feeder, and his friends. He also finally told him he felt sick at his stomach over having to move. A Froggy was kicking in the water, but he was listening. He remembered how it was when he had moved.

They sailed into a clear area. The sun made the water shimmer. Little groups of fish were chasing each other. The whole pond was aglow. All blue and green and aqua and gold.

A. Froggy pulled his lily pad beside E. Toad's. It seemed as if that big circle he had watched earlier had just reached out and brought him a friend. A. Toad thought, "I can't wait to go to school tomorrow!" The pond just shimmered and glowed in the bright sunlight.

It seemed
as if that big circle
had just reached out
and brought him a friend.

# I BELONG

"I wonder if my other mother would have done this," said T. Tiny Tadpole A' Thomas, often called T. Tiny.

Mama T. swallowed hard. "Well, I'm sure she would have," she said. They were making decorated flies for Christmas. You never knew when T. Tiny might ask such a question. Usually it was when just the two of them were doing something together like painting, or reading, or cooking. Some thought would click in T. Tiny's mind. She would get very quiet, her eyes would get a far-away look, and then out would pop a question!

T. Tiny had been adopted when she was 3 days old. Mama and Daddy T. told her about it at an early age. Mama T. began by telling her happy stories about adoption. Mama T. and Daddy T. felt this was much better than having some toad cousin or mean classmate, someone she thought was her friend, tell her.

E. Toad had been so excited when they brought T. Tiny Tadpole home. He and his aunt had met them at the door. He was just one big smile. He had water-colored a beautiful picture for T. Tiny. He set it on her bed. He loved her very much.

"Do you think my mother would have made Christmas flies?" T. Tiny Tadpole asked again.

"Yes, I do," answered Mama T. "She would have tried to do things to make you happy."

"Do you remember when we talked two days ago? I told you that you have a natural mother and an adoptive mother. You were born of your natural mother's body. You came from that mother's eggs."

T. Tiny answered as her eyes searched her Mother's face. "You said that for some reason my natural mother could not keep me and raise me through my tadpole time to my toad time."

"Yes," said Mama T. "I think that is real love. She was thinking of you. This mama you now have feeds you, clothes you, takes care of you when you are sick, and loves you very much also."

"I just wonder what she looks like," said T. Tiny quietly.

"I'm sure you do. I think I would wonder if I had been adopted. She must have been a very nice looking toad, for you are a beautiful tadpole!" Mama T. said with excitement.

T. Tiny put the icing on her last fly. Then she put tiny colored sprinkles made from Hummingbird nectar mixed with bright tints of flowers. This was held together with thin strips of lacy spider webs. T. Tiny looked at her flies; they were so beautiful! Mama T. looked at the kitchen; it was horrible! Sprinkles were everywhere: on the stove, on the counter, on the floor, and all over T. Tiny! When they made Christmas flies, it was a messy fun time!

"What a surprise!" said Daddy T. as he opened the door. "You have made so many beautiful flies." He would sample one and then another, letting his long tongue come out and lick the icing all around.

T. Tiny carefully placed all the iced flies in little piles saying, "These are for Mrs. Harry Toad, my teacher, and these are for Gran-Alice Toad, who is coming to visit, and these are for my friend, Linda Lop-Hop Toad.  And this big, bright, thick one is for E. Toad!"

E. Toad sat down with his big, bright, thick Christmas fly and licked all around it, swallowed it whole, strangled, coughed, sputtered and slobbered . . . then he threw up.  T. Tiny and Mama T. silently looked at him.  E. Toad often acted as if he had never had a bite to eat.

After T. Tiny played in her little rain-water pool, she crawled into her mossy bed.  Mama T. came in for the bedtime stories and prayers.

"Thanks for making Christmas flies with me," said T. Tiny.  "It was fun.  Don't forget we've got to do the paint brush flies tomorrow." This was T. Tiny Toad's very special recipe.  She loved to use her little feathered reed brush and paint the flies all different colors. After the good-night kiss, she went sound asleep.

The next day, E. Toad and T. Tiny were up early.  The cousin toads were coming and everything had to be ready.

Daddy T. was home because it was Saturday.  He and E. Toad

had been stacking sticks for the fireplace. They were taking a short rest when T. Tiny appeared in an old pink dance costume. She did a fast, little dance on a small round piece of wood, and they all laughed, for T. Tiny was always dressed in some costume. When they stopped laughing, T. Tiny was quiet for a few minutes.

"I wonder who my cousins might have been," she said quietly.

"Well, they could've been like Sandy Sue and Lisa Lou Toad," said Mama T. And they both laughed, for those two little toads were really giving T. Tiny a hard time. They were neighbors and everyday they were mad at T. Tiny for something. She never knew what!

Sometimes they said her book bag was too big, sometimes they made fun of her new shoes, sometimes they said they had heard she was adopted and wondered if she knew why she was "given away". One time they said that people don't love you if you are adopted. There were many times when T. Tiny was sad, but there were more times when she was MAD!

She tried to put Sandy Sue and Lisa Lou out of her mind. She blinked her eyes and said, "I surely would not have wanted those two

... T. Tiny appeared in an old costume.
They all laughed for T. Tiny was always
dressed in some outfit!

for my cousins," and then they were gone from her mind.

"You arrived in this family in a different way, but you are one of us," said Mama T.

"And all your cousins love you very much," said E. Toad.

T. Tiny rubbed her face against Daddy T.'s. Then she rubbed Mama T.'s face. She stood there for a few minutes.

"Why, I could have been in an orphanage right now," she exclaimed.

"Well, we're glad you aren't," said Daddy T. "You belong with us."

E. Toad reached over and pinched T. Tiny real hard.

"Mama, he pinched me and it really hurt," she hollered as she chased E. Toad from the family circle.

# THE FLIP-FLOP OF M. TURTLE TURNER

E. Toad, A. Froggy, and Z. Chameleon Achoo, his pet chameleon, were so bored!  The summer days were hot and loooooooonnnnnngggggg.  They had been swimming for hours just to stay cool.  Finally, feeling tired, they stretched out on the mossy bank and were sharing jokes.  A. Froggy could tell the funniest stories!

M. Turtle Turner, who was just one year old, floated by.  He turned his head the other way when he saw E. Toad and A. Froggy.

"Oh!  Man, he thinks he's something," said A. Froggy.  "He's always so grouchy and snaps at everybody."

"I wish he would never come out of the water," said E. Toad.

"He's stuck up.  Thinks he's about the coolest turtle around," said A. Froggy.

"I can hear you!" said M. Turtle sarcastically.

E. Toad and A. Froggy were surprised for they had been whispering.  Reeds and water must carry sounds!

"Well, we don't care if you can," they said together.  But really they did care because M. Turtle frightened them.  He was also bigger and could snap just like that!  And he had such a protective shell.  You could never make your hits hurt him.

M. Turtle got out of the water.  "I didn't realize you guys were the fighting kind.  But I guess you are," he said, making his eyes bounce back and forth . . . first at E. Toad . . . then at A. Froggy.  It was scary.  He shook the water off his shell.  He began to edge in closer . . . and . . . closer . . . and . . . closerandcloser.

Suddenly, one foot came up and over fell E. Toad.  Then M. Turtle's horny-edged jaw came down on A. Froggy's leg.  A. Froggy let out a big yell.  Mama T. came quickly hopping out the door.  She scanned the reeds and bulrushes.  Then she saw hands and legs flying.  "Oh dear," she thought.  "I must stop this."  But as she hopped closer she remembered Daddy T. saying, "let them settle it themselves."  She didn't like to see two against one, but M. Turtle was bigger so she stayed right where she was.

The hollering and wrestling continued for some time.  Then all was quiet.  Mama T. listened and watched E. Toad and A. Froggy as they hopped toward the house.  Mama T. met them.

"Whatever have you done to
M. Turtle Turner?" she asked.
"He's just resting" laughed A. Froggy.

"Whatever have you done to M. Turtle Turner?" she asked.

"He's just resting," laughed A. Froggy.

"I don't know what you mean," said Mama T. "Where is he resting?"

"It's not where he's resting, it's how he's resting," giggled E. Toad.

"O.K. I've had enough. Both of you come back to the pond with me," said Mama T. They hopped back to the tall weeds around the pond and there was M. Turtle lying on his back, desperately trying to turn over.

"How did he get this way?" asked Mama T.

"Well," said E. Toad, "A. Froggy got this stick, and we put it under M. Turtle. Then while A. Froggy held it in place, I hopped on it. M. Turtle just flipped right over. Serves him right. He thinks he's so smart."

"I don't care how he acts. You get a stick and flip him right back," said Mama T.

E. Toad and A. Froggy got a stick and tried the same trick, but the stick broke. Then they tied a long piece of grass to one foot and pulled. But they only twirled M. Turtle around! Achoo just scampered here and there, not knowing what to do.

"My neck is killing me!" exclaimed M. Turtle. "It is hanging out so far. I don't have a thing to prop it on." He was really afraid that if he pulled his head in his shell that he would never see daylight again! A big tear splashed down in the mud. E. Toad and A. Froggy looked at each other. They didn't feel so good right now. What was wrong? They should feel happy seeing M. Turtle so miserable. But they didn't. Something made their stomachs feel like butterflies were having a race inside.

"Let's tie a grape vine around him and pull him over," said Mama T.
"Tiny, Tiny, come here please and crawl under the edge of M. Turtle's shell," Mama T. called.
"Pull, pull," said E. Toad.
"Pull hard," said A. Froggy.
"All pull together, 1, 2, 3," said Mama T. And over came M. Turtle!

Mama T. patted his head and went to get marvelous gnat refreshments for everyone.

E. Toad knew in his heart that he should apologize, but it's so hard to tell another frog you are sorry. So he hopped around for a while and kept eating gnats when all of a sudden he said, "I'm sorry M. Turtle, that was a mean dirty trick."

30

"Our trick went too far," said A. Froggy.

"Well, I'm sorry too," said M. Turtle. "I did kinda think I could do anything. You guys put me in a situation where I couldn't do a thing!" They all laughed and ate the delicious gnats.

They got into the pond's cool water. A. Froggy and E. Toad were surprised that M. Turtle could swim so well. He showed them lots of tricks. M. Turtle seemed real nice inside that hard shell.

T. Tiny Tadpole said rather loudly, "Look! M. Turtle, your toes are webbed just like ours." E. Toad and A. Froggy were surprised. They had never thought about that.

"Guess you are one of us guys after all," said E. Toad. They climbed on a big rock and all jumped together into the pond's clear water.

# A VISIT TO HAPPY HOLLOW

E. Toad crossed and uncrossed his legs. He folded and unfolded his hands. He looked under his desk. He looked at the clock. Wouldn't the bell ever ring for school to be out? This had been the longest day of his life. He was tired, tired, tired. At last the bell! He grabbed his book bag and hopped for home at break-neck speed. His family was leaving tomorrow for a visit to Pattie Poo and Paw Paw Puddlejumper's. E. Toad's and his sister, T. Tiny Tadpole's grandparents lived far away. The trip seemed to take forever. It was too far to hop. A trip on the doodle bugs would be great! (Now Doodle Bugs are really called Lady Bugs, but the neighborhood of toads and frogs called them Doodle Bugs; all of them could not possibly be ladies!)

They left at dawn on a pack of shiny red doodle bugs.

Now you can do three things when you are traveling . . . eat, play games, and sleep. Sometimes they played games together, but often times they had problems. Take, for instance, the time E. Toad wanted to sleep and T. Tiny wanted to count ants. Every time he dozed, she would squeal, "I'm going to beat you Daddy T. I've got 50 more."

They left at dawn on a pack of shiny
red doodle bugs.

She usually kicked E. Toad at this time also. She didn't mean to; her little feet just flew out with delight at each hill of ants. E. Toad was so thankful when a cemetery finally appeared on her side, making her lose all of her ants. Daddy T. usually said, "Remember the rules of the game, T. Tiny?" She would pout anyway until she went to sleep.

The food sack was kept at Mama T.'s feet, and she passed out various snacks. Daddy T. usually ate all the way so the sack was being rattled every 15 minutes. T. Tiny Tadpole would ask, "Why does the food always live at Mama's feet?"

E. Toad would ask, "When does Daddy stop eating?"

E. Toad was plain worn out. His day at school had been so long. He fell asleep sitting straight up. He woke up as he heard the familiar song: "Going to See Paw Paw/Going to See Paw Paw/ yes, we are, yes we are/Going to See Paw Paw/Going to see Paw Paw/yes, we are, yes we are." Then Pattie's name was sung, then the aunts' and uncles', the cousins', then the pets. After that long song, the trip was over! They were there!

E. Toad and T. Tiny rushed in the cozy house in Happy Hollow. One Aunt T. and one Uncle T. and two cousins were already there. Such excitement! There was hugging and kissing and patting and laughter. T. Tiny Toad quickly hugged everyone. She went straight to the kitchen.

"Would they all be there?" she thought.

Of course they would . . . those delicious Katydid Krispies. T. Tiny squealed with joy because this time the Krispies were colored blue! They smelled so good. Nobody could make Krispies like Pattie Poo!

E. Toad disappeared with a cousin, but was soon called back. Here came another Aunt T. and Uncle T. and four more cousins. The hugging and kissing started all over again. A real joyful feeling seemed to surround that house in Happy Hollow.

Each family began to tell their news. The kid toads sat and listened for a while then someone yelled, "Let's go to the back porch and get that big box from under the day bed." There was a scramble as the eight cousins quickly hopped out of the door.

They got busy building a big farm with tiny acorns and sticks. It almost covered the entire floor. Each cousin was busy in a special area when Paw Paw walked through. All cousins set up straight and tried to say things that would please Paw Paw. E. Toad could remember when Paw Paw joked and laughed and chased them. Now he spent hours in his room.

Later that day E. Toad went to Paw Paw's room and stood by his desk.

"How are you, Paw Paw?" asked E. Toad.

"You'll know someday," answered Paw Paw in a quiet voice. Now that didn't mean a thing to E. Toad! But then Paw Paw smiled and gently tapped E. Toad with his hopping stick and E. Toad felt all warm inside. He kinda wanted to cry. He didn't know why. He decided to check the food drawer. There were no goodies! T. Tiny and the cousins had been there first! He patted Paw Paw and left.

As it began to get dark, the toad chorus assembled. Everyone, young and old, found their place and their singing part . . . that is, except T. Tiny. She continued to stand upside down right in the middle of the circle!

E. Toad thought, everyone needs to hear a toad chorus. It is amazing. First one book was used. Then another. Then one plays the piano, then another. The singing was LOUD, then soft, then

E. Toad thought "everyone needs to hear a toad chorus"

sad, 🙁 then happy, 🙂 then HIGH, then ʟᴏᴡ. Two would sing together, then three, then four. Paw Paw sang from his room; Pattie Poo sang and smiled at all those toads who were her own.

The melodies were pouring out when suddenly there was a loud shriek! The toads all jumped a mile high! "Where did that shriek come from?" asked a cousin. "It sounded as if it had come from under the big pine cone chair," answered Uncle Toad. They all stopped to look . . . there was T. Tiny with her webbed-out finger stuck in the tiniest hole.

She was crying and jerking on her fingers. The pine cone chair rocked as she pulled and twisted.

"I'll pat you, T. Tiny," said one cousin.
"I'll get some berry juice," said one Aunt T.
"I'll explain to Paw Paw," said another cousin.
"I'll crawl under and help get her fingers loose," said E. Toad.

He rubbed the little webbed-out fingers with berry juice until it was very wet. Then right out they came!

Mama T. thought how often those little fingers and toes of T. Tiny's got caught, stomped, jammed, or shoved into things where they didn't belong. Pattie Poo patted T. Tiny's head, Mama T. kissed her fingers, Daddy T. held her close, the aunts and uncles shook their heads. But the cousins and E. Toad made a big circle around her and swayed and sang. The awful scared feeling left her mind.

"Time for bed," the Aunt T. called. The cousins began pulling out sleeping bags of soft green moss. Pattie Poo added a quilt made of dried weeds and covered with leaves. Some had beautiful flowers dried and sewed into quilt squares. The room looked like one giant flower bed!

T. Tiny and two cousins about her age chose to rest with Pattie Poo for a while. Her stories were the greatest! Year after year grand toads slept with her. Year by year the same good stories were told. The grandtoads never got tired of them. Pattie and the grandtoads snuggled real close and the stories began. The first story was about a little pine tree. It got to keep its leaves all winter because it had been nice to a bird who wanted to live in its branches. T. Tiny could just see that smiling pine tree and that happy bird. As Pattie's voice hummed over them so low and soft, their eyes slowly closed.

The older cousins talked, played, ate, told stories, giggled and giggled. As the minutes added into hours, they began to get drowsy . . . all except E. Toad, who had to have another glass of Pattie Poo's boiled custard. When the first rays of sun danced in the early morning among the toad heads, the last eye closed and all was quiet at Pattie Poo's and Paw Paw's in Happy Hollow.

When the first rays of sun danced in among the toad heads, the last eye closed and all was quiet at Pattie Poo's and Paw Paw's in Happy Hollow.

There sat Achoo turning a beautiful golden green.
Do you see Achoo?

# Z. CHAMELEON ACHOO

E. Toad A' Thomas' chameleon had moved with the family when they left the patio brick wall. His name was Z. Chameleon Achoo. E. Toad called him Achoo. Achoo was such a good pet!

Sometimes when Achoo got excited he could change into many different colors. His big trick was changing colors when they were playing hide and seek. He would change from a beautiful lime green to a dusty brown and blend right into the pile of dead leaves.

One time Achoo laid down in some pine needles. E. Toad and his friend, A. Froggy Franklin, searched everywhere for him.

"Wheeeeere is that Achoo?" asked E. Toad.

"Please change colors so we can find you," said A. Froggy. Then, all of a sudden, A. Froggy said, "I see you . . . you fat pine needle!" A. Froggy had very sharp eyes. E. Toad liked to play with A. Froggy and Achoo. They never got mad at each other. They were pals.

Achoo always slept in the moss bed with E. Toad and they

cuddled close when the spring rains came.  They slept long hours when the snows fell.  They hopped and scampered many miles when the summer sun was bright.

One day Achoo was busy catching flies.  His long tongue would dart out and then go back in . . . just as fast as lightning.
On his tongue would be a delicious fly!  Down it went into his tummy.  He was so busy that he had wandered far away from E. Toad.

E. Toad called, "Achoo, Achoo," as he looked under rocks and in holes.

A. Froggy called, "Achoo, Achoo," as he searched in the flowers and weeds.

A. Froggy hopped to an open field.  There sat Achoo turning a beautiful golden green on a tall blade of grass.  The sun's hot rays were putting him to sleep.

All of a sudden a big Kitty K. came quickly into the field.  "I've got you now!" said Kitty K. as she pounced and swatted.

E. Toad and A. Froggy screamed and ran toward Achoo.  Achoo had seen Kitty K. just in time and had faded into the brightly colored grass. He tried not to breathe. Kitty K. was puzzled.

"Where is that chameleon?" she asked as she swatted and sprung at each moving thing.

Achoo saw his chance. He jumped down, turned brown on the dark ground and scampered to E. Toad and A. Froggy. All three dashed for a hole where the doodlebugs lived. The Doodles wouldn't mind their quick entrance for they were friends.

E. Toad hugged Achoo. "Don't you ever get lost again," he said. "That Kitty K. nearly got you," said A. Froggy.

Achoo just licked their faces as he tried to slow down his quick breaths and his fast heart beats.

"He's had enough excitement for today," said E. Toad as he watched Achoo put his head under a rock and go to sleep.

E. Toad had birthdays and he grew! Achoo had birthdays also. Their play times changed. The races had slowed down. The hide and seek times were spent lying on the moss. E. Toad, A. Froggy and M. Turtle played with sets of army toads. GI Toad and his field hospital was spread everywhere.

Often times E. Toad noticed that Achoo moved so slowly and slept a lot.

"Are you bored, Achoo?" asked E. Toad.
"He's a lazy chameleon," said A. Froggy.

"He's changing colors; he must be dreaming about all of our fun times!" said M. Turtle.

Achoo turned rusty brown, but stayed sound asleep.

One morning after E. Toad had left for school, Mama T. glanced in Achoo's pen. Achoo was very still. Mama T. hopped closer. Achoo did not seem to be breathing. She had watched E. Toad tell Achoo goodbye that morning. Achoo had seemed weak and slow.

"Oh! My goodness," said Mama T. aloud for she knew Achoo was dead.

Mama T. had a quick thought. Why not take Achoo and bury him? No, she said to herself. E. Toad will want to tell him goodbye.

I'll take him inside the house. She laid Z. Chameleon Achoo on his little mossy bed and covered him with a blanket of thin cobwebs.

E. Toad came home from school and, as usual, went straight to Achoo's pen.

"Mother," he called, "where is Achoo?"

Mother T. hopped to E. Toad. "I have taken Achoo inside. I checked on him this morning and Achoo had died," she said quietly.

E. Toad turned quickly away from Mama T. He ran inside and put his head down by Achoo.

Mama T. put her arm around E. Toad and said, "You had many fun-filled days with Achoo. You were kind to him. You took good care of him. He was a special pet because you made him feel so special."

E. Toad wanted Achoo to come back. He cried and cried, and then he cried some more. He could not live without Achoo! He would never feel good again.

"I'll never, never have another pet. They make your heart hurt," he said as he went out the door to tell A. Froggy.

For days E. Toad A' Thomas and A. Froggy Franklin sat and did nothing. When they did talk, they talked about Achoo. They put flowers on his grave and sat right down with the flowers and cried some more.

"Do you think we should get E. Toad another pet?" asked Mama T. one day when E. Toad had seemed very sad.

"He does seem lonesome," answered Daddy T. "But I think we should wait."

"I do hate to see him miss Achoo so much, but I, too, believe we should wait," she said.

The days crept by. E. Toad was glad he could bring Achoo to his mind in an instant!

But one night, many months later, E. Toad had a strange experience. E. Toad and A. Froggy were spending the night together. E. Toad sat straight up in the bed!

"I can't remember what Achoo looks like!" he screamed. "Sometimes I can't either," said A. Froggy.

"I don't believe this! I thought I would never forget. I don't like this," said E. Toad.

"Neither do I," said A. Froggy.

They sat quietly for a while. Then A. Froggy reached over and tickled E. Toad. They were soon practicing their toad-kwan-do holds they had learned in wrestling class. They were very still in their tight holds when suddenly E. Toad let go. A. Froggy fell right off the bed! Their laughter filled the twigs and roots and moss that was their home. Friends are fun to have around, thought E. Toad.

Fall came early that year. The leaves fell around E. Toad. He studied their colors . . . red like hot fire . . . yellow like the sun turning into melted butter . . . orange like pumpkins . . . brown like dirt. The summer sun was gone. The flowers and birds were going away.

"Fall makes me sad," said E. Toad. "The earth seems to be saying goodbye to us."

Mama T., who was busy thinking about fall clothes for E. Toad and his sister, T. Tiny, stopped sewing. "Listen to this poem my mama taught me," she said. Mama T. remembered almost every word of the poem about the bright, blue skies of October. "The month of June is hot sun and green leaves. The month of October is blue, blue skies and leaves of bright colors of gold and rust and red," she said. E. Toad thought about this. It was both a happy and sad time.

School started and E. Toad and T. Tiny were excited! There were many things that had to be done in school and after school . . . lessons in gymnastics and dancing, ball games, and band practice. And homework!

Daddy T. came home early one night. His eyes were shining and twinkling. His face looked happy with a smile spread from ear to ear. Daddy T. sat a big acorn on the table.

"E. Toad, please come here," he called.
E. Toad hopped to the table.

"Open the acorn," said Daddy T.

E. Toad opened it quickly and peeked inside. He squealed with delight. Inside was a cute little salamander. It jumped and tried to hide when E. Toad squealed.

"Oh! So black . . . and so shiny," said E. Toad as he reached to pick up the little salamander. He held the wiggling one close to him. Out came a little tongue and wiped E. Toad across the face! The family laughed as E. Toad and his new pet looked at each other.

"It's a little girl," said Daddy T.
"Oh! Good," said E. Toad. "I'm going to name her C. Salamander Smith and call her C. Sal."

"That is a very good name," said Mama T.
"I need a pet. I need a pet!" said T. Tiny as she rubbed C. Sal.

"You are about old enough to care for one," said Mama T. as she patted T. Tiny.

Black night came. There were no stars to be seen in the dark sky. But E. Toad and C. Sal were shining in their soft moss bed. Their heads were together. So were their hearts.

SUGAR

"Open the acorn"
said Daddy T.
E. Toad opened it quickly
and peeked inside.
He squealed with
delight! Inside was
a cute little
              salamander.
"oh! so black and shiny"

CARE
of
PETS

Gnats

C. Sal

Stars seemed to be twinkling around them.  The glow sent golden star dust  everywhere.

# THE GHOST

"I'm going out to play," said T. Tiny Tadpole A' Thomas. She hopped out the back door.

"Well, don't be out after dark," said Mama T. "You know you were late the last two or three times."

Mama T. walked to the door. "T. Tiny, do you hear me? DO NOT BE LATE. There are many dogs, cats and snakes out at night."

"I hear you, Mom. I won't be late," said T. Tiny.

It was mid-afternoon and Mama T. had much to do before suppertime. She was pickling minnows to have during the cold months when the pond was frozen. T. Tiny and E. Toad had done their chores for the day, so she was really glad for the time alone. She needed the quiet so she could concentrate on the recipe for preparing minnows.

She thought about how forgetful T. Tiny had been lately. Mama T. had spent some time talking with her about this problem. T. Tiny seemed to always be thinking about other things as they talked. T. Tiny's mind ran full-speed ahead with her active little body. Their latest conversations came to her mind.

"Did you put your clothes away?"
"I forgot."
"Have you brushed your gums, T.Tiny?"
"I forgot."
"Why are you coming home so late?"
"I forgot."

Surely T. Tiny would remember to come home on time today.

The minutes seemed to have flown into hours. Before Mama T, knew it, the sun's rays were deeply slanted. She placed the last minnow in the walnut shell and clamped it together tightly. She dipped it in some real hot water and it was sealed, ready for a delicious dinner much later in the winter. Now her canning was done. Mama T. flopped on the toad stool before beginning supper.

She heard E. Toad and his friends gathered in the yard for a few more minutes of fun.

Quickly the night fell. A stillness surrounded the house. Mama T. went to the door to look for T. Tiny. E. Toad came in and went to his room.

The lightning bugs that were kept inside for light had not turned on their brightness. All was dark inside and out.

Mama T. called loudly, "T. Tiny, T. Tiny. Come home." But she didn't hear an answer at all. She began to start the dinner meal, but she remained uneasy. She hopped to the door quite often and called, "T. Tiny, T. Tiny."

It was very dark now. Mama T. asked E. Toad if he would hop around the oak tree block and see if he could find T. Tiny. E. Toad hopped out; Mama T. continued to check at the door.

E. Toad had been gone just a few minutes when Mama T. heard voices. She recognized one voice as T. Tiny's. The other voices were of older neighborhood kid toads. They were laughing and joking.

Mama T. felt her anger rising. The group approached the house. Mama T. quickly grabbed a sheet of cobwebs she had sewn together for a thin blanket. She threw it over her head. She heard T. Tiny holler "goodbye" and open the door. Just as she did, Mama T. stood up. T. Tiny screamed like she had never screamed before. She slammed the door shut! She hopped quickly back to her friends.

"There's a ghost in there!  There's a ghost in there!" she yelled. Roger Race Toad laughed.  "There's no such thing as ghosts." "There is.  There is.  You come look," said T. Tiny.

Roger Race Toad puffed himself up real big.  He was the oldest of the group.  He really needed to show that he was fearless and strong.  "Come on," he said.  He pushed ahead of the group.

Mama T. sat down on a toad stool just inside the door.  Roger Race Toad opened the door.  Mama T. slowly stood up with arms and hands stretched out far. The spider webs clung to her and a lightning bug had landed on her web just as she stood.  Her entire appearance took on an eerie glow.  Roger let out a blood-curdling scream.  He fell backward out the door.  The other toads fell back like dominoes.

Mama T. did not want to frighten them out of their wits.  She removed the spider web covering. She hopped to the door just as they were scrambling up to jump away.

"Mama, Mama, was that you?" screamed T. Tiny.

"Yes, I am your ghost!  I'm sorry that I frightened you.  That was a

Mama T. quickly grabbed a sheet of cobwebs she had sewn together for a thin blanket. She threw it over her head.

bad scare, I know.  When you are late, I get afraid that something has happened to you.  We both have really given each other shivers and **shakes**," Mama T. said as she squeezed T. Tiny close to her and kissed her little face.

"Now you other kid toads get on home.  Your mothers will be worried.  It's much too late to be out," said Mama T.

"You are the best ghost I've ever seen," said Roger Race Toad. "You nearly scared me to death."

They were all laughing when E. Toad returned.  After he heard the story, he said to T. Tiny, "I'll bet you won't be out after dark again."

T. Tiny Tadpole thought to herself (No, I will not be late again) and she wasn't!

# TOAD TIMES IN THE SMOKIES

It was pouring down rain. But it felt good to E. Toad A' Thomas' warm, dry skin.

What a good day for a camping trip to begin. Toads love to travel in the rain. The rain keeps them moist. They can travel great distances when the weather is cool.

E. Toad and his sister, T. Tiny, had been looking forward to this trip for a lllllllooooooooonnnnnnnnngggggg time. They loved to camp and every summer the A' Thomases took a vacation.

The family had been studying books and maps for days. They finally decided on a prairie campsite . . . but A. Froggy Franklin's family said it was much too hot and dry!

Then they picked a place near Niagara Falls, but M. Turtle Turner's family said it was much too cold. Why they had to stay in their shells the entire time!

Finally the A' Thomases decided on a nice spot right in the Smoky Mountains. It had cool streams, mossy banks, sunbathing rocks, and tall, lacy ferns. Best of all, insects were everywhere. What a feast they would have! E. Toad could just see himself lounging under a big fern and catching insects all day with his long, sticky tongue. He would probably have to share with T. Tiny though. She was always too busy to sit for long!

"I'll get the kitchen equipment and the food ready," said Mama T. "I'll get the sleeping bags and quilts," said E. Toad.

"I'll get the toys and books," said T. Tiny as she made numerous trips from her room and E. Toad's to the camper.

"I'll pack the camper," said Daddy T. "But I'll have to work and work to make everything fit!"

"T. Tiny, T. Tiny," he said. "You can't bring anything else. The fun box is full!"

Soon the family was on its way. Tadpole dolls that T. Tiny called her polliwogs, digging shovels, hacking-hatches, games and books, and dragonfly snacks were hidden in every nook and cranny inside the camper.

"I'm so glad my red lantern did not get left," said E. Toad. "We'll need it at our campsite."

After days of traveling and staying at campsites along the way, they arrived at the Great Smoky Mountains National Park.

"I like this campsite with the big rocks around it," said E. Toad.
"I like this one with all the tiny mountain flowers," said T. Tiny.

"Each camping place is better than the one we just passed," said Mama T. "This is a hard decision."

"Well, let's just hurry up! I'm hungry," said Daddy T.

Finally, they all voted on the one among the tall ferns. A mountain stream was just behind the ferns. It was filled with large boulders, medium-sized rocks, and tiny stones.

"What a place for splashing," said T. Tiny as she jumped into the low cool pool, sending great drops of water all over everyone!

"What a lovely, relaxing place," said Mama T. and Daddy T. together. "We will have some quiet, peaceful days," said Daddy T. "And we won't have to worry about Kitty K. at all," Mama T. said happily.

E. Toad and Daddy T. collected sticks.  They made a warm campfire using E. Toad's Magic Breath, as they all called it.  Many times the fire would be almost gone and E. Toad would use his Magic Breath and flames would raise their heads and begin to pop and snap.

Mama T. and T. Tiny fixed the best supper they had ever eaten,   fried bush crickets.

"Why are you so hungry when you eat outside?" asked E. Toad.

"The cool mountain breeze, the sound of water going over rocks, the smell of crickets frying.  These all make you hungry," said Daddy T.

"You two haven't just been sitting here you know," said Mama T.  "You have been hopping and jumping and splashing and swimming and climbing and ducking and diving.  That kind of exercise makes your body want more food."

"But it all tastes different," said T. Tiny.  "Crickets are yummy out here.  At home, they are yucky!"  Mama T smiled as she looked at T. Tiny's cricket-smeared face.

Mama T. was a little concerned about the camper beds.  "I'm

afraid T. Tiny might roll out and onto the ground," she said.

"That cannot happen with the tent top fastened very tightly under the bed.  There is no way T. Tiny can fall out," said Daddy T.

"I'll catch her," said E. Toad as he pushed his webbed-feet against her toad stool, rocking it.

After a few more songs around the campfire, they all felt very tired.  Soon they were fast asleep.

In the middle of the night a little voice said, "Mama, Mama!"

Mama T. sat straight up.  "Where is that voice coming from?" she asked herself.

"Mama, Mama!" it said again.
Mama T. and Daddy T. both hopped up.

"It's T. Tiny's voice," said Mama T., "but where is she?  She sounds far away.  She's not in her bed!"

Mama T. and Daddy T. hurried out the door.  There under the camper lay T. Tiny!

"How could she have gotten out?" asked Daddy T. in a very quiet, low voice.

"T. Tiny Tadpole can get out of anything!" said Mama T. as she brushed leaves and dirt off T. Tiny.

"T. Tiny, are you OK?" asked E. Toad anxiously.

In her little frightened voice she said, "I'm OK, but it is a long way down. It was scary."

They all hugged and kissed her.

Soon she had settled down for the night right between Mama and Daddy T.

The next day when the sun began to creep in among the tall oak trees, the A' Thomases were already up and ready for their hop-hike. They ate snacks as they listened to the ranger, Frog Forest Feather-Fur, explain about how this part of the earth was formed. They saw many different plants and trees and flowers. They looked in their guide books and tried to remember the names of these mountain plants.

"Now I need to tell you about black snakes," said Frog Forest

Feather-Fur. "This is their home, but if you leave your food out, they'll move into your home! Do not try to feed them your snacks. Do not try to get close to them. Keep your food locked up and away from them. That's my best advice."

"Do you think we'll see a black snake?" asked T. Tiny.

"I doubt it," said E. Toad. "Sometimes they do slither around, but they'll leave us alone if we do what Frog Forest Feather-Fur said."

The sun was going down when they returned to their campsite. It had been a very long, interesting day. They just fell in their warm sleeping bags. They were tired. They were sleepy. They were happy.

Mama T. woke up in the middle of the night and went to get a drink of water. She returned to the camper and, as she lay down, she heard a strange noise outside. She looked outside of the camper just as a big, black snake slithered to the neighboring campsite.

"Wake up! Wake up," she said to Daddy T. Their eyes nearly popped out of their heads. They all watched as the snake wound itself around the neighbor's nut chest and popped it open. He then ate everything in it and traveled on to the next campsite.

The next morning the campground was all excited.

"Did the black snake visit you?" asked one of the campers.

"No, thank goodness. He just slid through. We saw his path," said Daddy T.

Another family said, "He ate every bit of our food!"
The A' Thomases were so glad they had put all of their food away.

The next door neighbors were nowhere to be seen! Frog Forest Feather-Fur said they had left early that morning before the sun came up. They had been very frightened when they saw the big black snake break into their nut chest. Snakes do eat frogs and toads, so they all felt lucky that the snake had not harmed anyone.

The campground finally settled down. The A' Thomases spent the days hop-hiking, swimming, visiting new places and eating gobs of insects.

E. Toad carved sticks with his little knife and spent hours in the mountain stream.

T. Tiny often disappeared, but could always be found visiting

She looked out of the camper just as a big black snake slithered to the neighboring campsite. "WAKE UP! WAKE UP!

with other camping families.  One day Mama T. missed her and called her name, "T. Tiny, T. Tiny, where are you?"  Just then E. Toad spotted T. Tiny's pink striped umbrella bobbing up and down as she led a merry pack of kid toads through all the mud puddles.

E. Toad and T. Tiny loved these camping days.  They put all the memories of these happy times away in their hearts and heads.  The vacation seemed to pass quickly, and soon they were back at the marsh around the pond.

"Boy!  Does that old pond look good," said E. Toad.

He hollered to A. Froggy and M. Turtle, "Come on you two.  Let's hit that cool, clear water.  It's never looked so good!"

A. Froggy brought C. Sal.  He kept C. Sal for his friend while the A' Thomases were on vacation.  E. Toad hugged C. Sal.  T. Tiny came running, and they all plunged into the pond.  They were glad to be back at home.

# THE FLYING FROGS OF FAR AWAY LAND

The Flying Frogs had spent many months trying to get out of a far away land.

Their homes and lives were being destroyed because of a long war. The news, over the Frog and Toad network (FTN) showed many pictures of these sad frogs. But the first time E. Toad A' Thomas and his sister, T. Tiny Tadpole, really heard about it was at church. A family of tree frogs had escaped their ruined land. They needed a group of frogs to sponsor them and help them get settled into their new homes. First Pond Church had agreed to do this.

"They don't speak our language," said E. Toad. "How can they go to school over here?"

"Well, that's something they will have to learn. I'm sure it will be hard for them to have to start all over in a very different country," said Mama T. "They will need our love and support."

After a long journey, the Big Swallow Tail landed. Out came the Flying Frogs. The A' Thomases would never forget the looks on their faces. Their eyes were open so wide. So were their smiles.

All the church toads were happy.  E. Toad and T. Tiny put their arms around the flying frog children for the first time.  They felt a love for them that they would never forget.

A newly decorated house among the reeds was perfect.  Low limbs from surrounding trees made good landing places for the flying frogs.  The family soon began to learn new ways and customs.

"Tell us about how you used to live," said E. Toad.

"Tell us about everything," said T. Tiny.
They were really strange frogs.  They could arch their bodies, spread out the wide webbing beneath their fingers and toes and glide over to a limb 35 feet away!

"Now that takes some getting used to," said E. Toad.
"And their feet are so funny!" said T. Tiny.

"What is that sticky stuff like glue that spreads out over the webbed circle?" asked E. Toad.

"Why that keeps us from falling," said one of the kid flying frogs, as she walked straight up a tree!

They really were strange frogs. They
could arch their bodies, spread out the
wide webbing between their fingers and
toes and glide over to a limb 35 feet away.

Another one said, "Look at this," as she walked upside down on the limb and didn't fall off.

E. Toad and T. Tiny were amazed!

"Their house smells so different from ours. What is it? It's not a bad smell . . . just strong and different."

Mama T. explained that they often cooked with a sauce brought from the far away land. They used it on all of their insects . . . fried, baked, or boiled!

"They are so quiet," said T. Tiny.

"They are having to learn a lot of new things," said Daddy T. "They have to think and think."

The Flying Frogs told of many happy times in their far away land. They also told of many unhappy, frightening times. Everyone tried to help them forget some of those bad times. They helped the family become a part of the pond community. The Flying Frogs were loved and accepted.

It was such an interesting time for Daddy T. and Mama T. as they watched the Flying Frog children begin to laugh and play. The Flying Frog mother, Fun Frog, and Mama T. became close friends. They shared many joys as Mama T. went with Fun Frog to shop and took her to classes for learning about her new country. She introduced her to other new friends. The Flying Frog father was working very hard at his new job. He had been a Flying Frog Fighter in the army. He had to learn a new way of life.

T. Tiny said, "May we have the Flying Frogs over to trick or treat on Halloween?"

"Why, yes, that would be fun," said Mama T. and she immediately began to think about costumes for all four flying frog kids.

Daddy T. hopped with them as they went through the pond neighborhood. They squeaked with delight over all of their surprises. They shared and swapped goodies for hours.

"This is the most fun we've ever had!" they said in a high Flying Frog chorus.

"You know what?" said T. Tiny one day. "These Flying Frogs are so different from us on the outside. But on the inside we all seem to be the same.  The same things that make me happy, make them happy."

"And the same things that make me sad make them sad.  They have feelings just like we do!" said E. Toad.

The Flying Frog children joined Mama T.'s kid choir at the church.  T. Tiny was so surprised!

"Mama, they can sing just like we can!  And in our language," she exclaimed.

One beautiful day the Flying Frog children sang a song of thanks for their new country at a church service.  Many happy tears flowed in the Toad congregation as they listened to their sweet voices.

Fun Frog got very sick and died in this new land.  The heart break, the deep hurt, and sorrow surrounded them all.

"Why did God let this happen?" asked E. Toad.  "Fun Frog was such a good amphibian."

"She wanted to live here in her new home.  She wanted to see her four kid frogs grow up," said T. Tiny.

Dr. Fredrick Frog, the minister at First Pond Church, said, "Sadness, pain, accidents, and yes, death, comes to us all . . . bad and good toads." The kind minister continued, "The kid frogs will continue on their journey through life because Fun Frog taught them many good things to help prepare them. They will be OK."

Although E. Toad and T. Tiny were very sad, they did hear what Dr. Fredrick Frog said, and although it was hard to understand, they kept it in their heads and put the goodness of God in their hearts.

# THE BIG JUMP

E. Toad A' Thomas got up early on Friday and hurried to the glimmer glow . . . the part of the pond that was very clear. It sent back good and bad reflections! He could hardly believe that the warts were still there!

Mama T. had said, "If you really wish something and think on it hard enough, it would come to pass . . . most of the time!" This could not be true. He had wished and wished . . . hoping these warts would leave. But they were still there. Just all over him!

It would make him feel better if his friend, A. Froggy Franklin, had them too, but frogs don't have warts like toads. His skin was as clear as could be. And here was E. Toad with warts, warts, warts!

He hopped back to the house and said in a mean voice to Mama T., "No, I don't want any insects, earthworms, minnows or spiders for breakfast." He might never eat again.

He went to his moss bed. He pulled the spider web comforter over his head. Then he said out loud, "Who wants to hop around with warts all over you? I'll lose all of my friends!" He felt too big to cry. But the tears came anyway.

Just then his mother gently pulled the comforter back and said, "Those warts are really bothering you, aren't they?"

"Go away Mama T.," he thought. He buried himself deeper in the moss.

"When you feel better, E. Toad, I want to tell you about a contest at the YTCA that Dad told me about."

He gave a big sigh. "Both Mom and Dad try to be so cheerful when things are not good in my life. They think things up for me to do when I really just want to be left alone."

The gloom stayed with him all day. When school was finally out he raced home. He did not want to hop along slowly with A. Froggy and M. Turtle. He wanted to be all by himself.

On his bed lay a pamphlet about a jumping contest being held in about two months. He read it, then flipped it up in the air. "Who cares about a contest?" he thought. He knew that frogs could out-jump anyone except maybe a kangaroo. His friend had told him that he was a good jumper, but the contest just didn't interest him.

He went outside and sat staring into space. Then, all of a

sudden, he just jumped right over a toad stool. For some reason jumping and not even touching the toad stool gave him a big thrill!

He hopped back to the tree. He thought he would see just how far he could jump. He saw a rock and said, "OK, that's my line." To his amazement he almost jumped even with the rock! So he tried it again. This time his jump was even with the rock! He moved the rock a little farther away and he jumped again . . . almost there . . . another jump . . . he was there!

This couldn't be true. He was really jumping high and far! He practiced for a whole hour that day, and when he went to bed, he went right to sleep. His dreams were fantastic. He jumped all night. Why, he even jumped over the moon!

The next day was Saturday. He usually slept a little later, but he was awake bright and early. He could hardly wait to see how far he could jump that day. He practiced and practiced. He hardly stopped for lunch. He continued to move the rock farther away. He stretched every muscle to make the jump.

He learned that if he got real close to the ground and pulled his legs up tight under him that it made a powerful spring. He crouched lower and lower. And he sprang higher and higher. He was so tired that he fell over on a pine straw mound.  He drifted into a light sleep.

He awoke in the late afternoon.  He was so sore that he could hardly hop home.  He bathed in the hollow little pool behind his house.  He had fried flies for supper.  He really loved friend flies.  He went straight to bed.  And for that whole day he never once thought about all those warts!

E. Toad kept up this routine for days and weeks.  A. Froggy and M. Turtle couldn't imagine what had happened to him.  He never wanted to play Froggy-In-The-Mill-Pond, or catch flies, or do anything but jump.

E. Toad kept on practicing.  He asked his dad to help him.  Together they worked for days and weeks.  Before he knew it the day of the big contest had arrived.

He was frightened over this event.  He was just plain scared when he saw those big bullfrogs take their places.  He felt weak and sick.  He legs felt like rubber.  I can never jump that far . . . Never! . . . Never!

Just then he saw Daddy T. standing to the side of the jump range.  Daddy T. gave him a wink and an OK sign.  Right then he felt the strength come back into his legs!

As the announcer said, "ready," he crouched low.  As he said, "set," he bounced up and down.  As he said, "go," he sprang forward as never before!

E. Toad stayed in that place for the measurement, but he knew that he had won because he saw A. Froggy do a backwards somersault.  He only did that when he was the very happiest!

The announcer slowly read:
"Boom Boom Bullfrog---1 foot, 11 inches
Tim Toad---1 foot
M. Molly Hop---1 foot, 8 & 1/2 inches
Tadpole Topper Green---4 inches
Happy Hopper Green---1 foot, 6 inches
E. Toad A' Thomas---2 feet!"

Why, the farthest jump ever recorded was 2 feet, 8 inches.  And a big bullfrog had accomplished that!  He couldn't believe it.  He had really surprised himself!

He received his beautiful trophy while the crowd clapped and clapped.  His family and friend patted and hugged and praised him.  He had such a good feeling.

As the announcer said "ready," he crouched low. As he said "set," he bounced up and down. As he said "go," he sprang forward as never before.

When he lay in bed that night and said his prayers, he promised that he would keep jumping. He could beat the 2 feet, 8 inches record! In his dreams, he saw the world go spinning around. He made a great big jump and went right over the world!

**(VERY HIGH VOICE)**

CREAK, CREAK...**CROAK, CROAK**

**(VERY LOW VOICE)**

"Did you see that?" E Toad A' Thomas asked his friend, A. Froggy Franklin.

"Yes, I did.  What do you suppose is happening to B. Bullfrog Brown?" A. Froggy replied.

"Well, I don't know, but it surely does look strange.  And listen to that deep croak.  He's never sounded like that before," said E. Toad.

B. Bullfrog Brown was sitting by the pond's edge on a log and his throat had suddenly gotten very LARGE.  Then out came a deep croaking sound.  It looked just like he had swallowed a big balloon.  B. Bullfrog was a few months older, but he was a friend and neighbor. He was always very nice to E. Toad.  E. Toad liked him.

E. Toad continued to look at B. Bullfrog.  He had noticed lately that when B. Bullfrog talked, his voice cracked.  It went way up high and then way down low.  Was this going to happen to him, he wondered? Maybe B. Bullfrog had a disease that he might catch.  Maybe he might die. He looked at A. Froggy. He looked frightened also.

"Did you see that?"

E. Toad asked his friend
A. Froggy... B. Bullfrog Brown
was sitting on a log by the
pond's edge and his throat had
suddenly gotten very LARGE.

"Come on, let's go over to my house and get in our hole and read," said A. Froggy.

"OK, let me tell Mama T. where I'll be," said E. Toad.

E. Toad and A. Froggy hopped away from each other, but their thoughts were still together and on B. Bullfrog Brown!

These were long, lazy times when the days were so hot that E. Toad could hardly stay out of the pond. The sun seemed to be so close. No rain had fallen in weeks. Toads and frogs don't like dry weather for long spells. They usually spend their days in damp holes. E. Toad liked this new, mossy, cool hole that he and A. Froggy had found. They had been spending most of the long days in the hole, reading. Mama T. seemed so surprised when E. Toad had been announcing lately that he was going to A. Froggy's to read.

"To read!" she said. "Well, that's unusual for you, E. Toad. You usually are playing leap-frog, or swimming, or resting at the pond's edge. You reading time is usually at night when you can't go outside. What have you found to read that is so interesting?"

"Oh, nothing much," replied E. Toad. "Just some old books from A. Froggy's attic." He hopped out before any more questions could be asked.

On his way to A. Froggy's, he stopped at M. Turtle Turner's, but he was with his girlfriend.

"How silly," thought E. Toad, "to be with a girl when he could be spending time with the boys."

M. Turtle, being older, didn't seem to have as much time for him and A. Froggy as he used to. He always wanted to stop by his girlfriend's house. Sometimes M. Turtle just lay in a grape vine hammock and listened to music. Sometimes he just slept.

E. Toad arrived at A. Froggy's and they slid into their hole. "It really is nice in here," E. Toad thought. "I must make sure that T. Tiny doesn't find this secret place. She would move in all of her troll dolls and then the teaching supplies that she lugged everywhere. Oh, goodness! She might move in her Easy Bake Oven."

"Hey, E. Toad, look at this," exclaimed A. Froggy. He handed him a book that showed a female frog laying eggs. The next picture showed a male frog fertilizing them. Under the pictures was the word, REPRODUCTION. E. Toad looked and studied the pictures. Reproduction means: how animals and plants produce new individuals. They looked at each other and then broke into hysterical laughter.

"Well, I don't believe I got here that way," said A. Froggy.

"I know I didn't!" said E. Toad.

"Look at this picture. It shows the eggs on the mother's back," said A. Froggy.

"That is gross and unbelievable," said E. Toad.

"And this says that some kinds of tree frogs carry their eggs on the male's leg," exclaimed A. Froggy.

E. Toad shut his eyes. "Maybe if I think real hard I'll understand this---better yet, maybe it will go away!"

He started to say something to A. Froggy and his voice made a funny low croaking sound. A. Froggy collapsed with laughter.

"Don't laugh," said E. Toad. "This is not funny. My throat may be very sick. Maybe the next thing to happen will be that big throat like B. Bullfrog Brown."

E. Toad lay in the moss. A. Froggy continued to flip the pages of the book.

"Look at this!" laughed A. Froggy, and shoved the book over to E. Toad. There, before them, right in this book, was a picture of a toad. His throat looked just like B. Bullfrog's. Under the picture it said, "Mating Season."

Now he was confused. He needed someone to explain this to him. E. Toad hopped right out of the hole and started home. He didn't even say good-bye to A. Froggy. Anyway, A. Froggy was holding his stomach and laughing beyond control.

E. Toad could hardly choke down his food at dinner. He wished T. Tiny would hurry up and go to bed so he could talk to Daddy T.

When he was sick, he needed Mama T. But tonight he needed to talk to Daddy T. When they worked and played together, they often had good talks. Anyway, he hoped he wasn't sick!

At last T. Tiny went to bed. Mama T. was folding clothes. E. Toad asked his father to come outside. As they sat on the toad stools around the picnic table, E. Toad began to tell Daddy T. about the pictures in the book, about his voice cracking and then about B. Bullfrog Brown. Daddy T. sat quietly and listened. Then he smiled.

"E. Toad, what is just beginning to happen to you is a very

normal thing. It's all a part of growing up. Your body begins to change in lots of small ways. One of the first ways is that your voice changes from higher tones to lower tones. It will soon stop its cracking and you'll end up with a low male voice."

"Is this normal?" asked E. Toad.

"Yes, very normal. All toads and frogs go through this. It's a preparation time for a later stage when you are ready to mate and raise your own kid toads."

"Is B. Bullfrog there?" asked E. Toad.

"He's just beginning in the mating stage. His throat makes a big balloon so that his mating call can be heard far away."

"Who is listening?" asked E. Toad.

"Why girl toads are changing too, and they are listening for the mating call," said Daddy T.

"I got afraid when I saw B. Bullfrog," said E. Toad. "I know we've talked about some of these changes before, but I didn't know it would actually happen to me."

"It happens to everyone. It's normal. It's natural. Keep asking questions. And before long you will be noticing those cute little female toads!" said Daddy T. with a twinkle in his eye and a smile on his face. "That's a big change that will happen," he added.

"Oh no!" said E. Toad, "Not to me."

The summer passed. The long cold winter froze the pond. Then spring arrived. The pond ice melted. The lily pads in the pond turned bright green and flower buds appeared. New growth was everywhere. Why E. Toad had even grown an inch when he measured!

E. Toad first noticed Tammy

Toad Tolbert on a bright spring day. He kinda winked at her. She smiled back at him. He waited for her after school and they hopped around the pond together- not one, not two, but three times until the sky was beginning to change colors for sundown.

E. Toad didn't know why he felt so good! Just happy and carefree! He looked at the big pond. It glimmered and glowed brightly in the sun. It was making a merry rippling sound kinda like his rapidly beating heart.

E. Toad first noticed Tammy Toad Tolbert on a
bright Spring day. He Kinda winked at her. She
smiled back at him. They hopped around the pond
together - not one - not two, but three times until the
sky was changing to all different colors for sundown.

# EPILOGUE

And so E. Toad and T. Tiny hopped on through life. There were other moves and many other pets. There were good friends and not-so-good friends. The grandparents died . . . the house in Happy Hollow changed. The cousins scattered, but kept in touch. T. Tiny located her birth mother and father, but considered them friends, not parents.

They each met many challenges in life. Sometimes they succeeded. Sometimes they did not. They developed their own value system and philosophy toward life.

Their family times together were often spent reminiscing about these years of happy and sad incidents. These times are gone . . . but not forgotten.

E. Toad and T. Tiny were deeply loved.

# BIBLIOGRAPHY

--Lamb, Wally, I Know This Much Is True, Regan Books(a division of Harper Collins), NY, 1998.

--For some of the drawings I used ideas from the children's magazine, "Ranger Rick", published by The National Wildlife Federation, USA.

--the drawing of T. Tiny in costume was inspired by a greeting card from American Greetings.

--the pond photo was taken by Drake Sharp, or as he's also known, E. Toad A' Thomas, on the road to Vidalia, GA.

# ACKNOWLDEGEMENTS

First, I want to thank my friend, Dale Nicholson, for her insistence that I have a publisher read my story. She even pushed me into a first lunch with Bill and Bo. She has always given me her full support in many areas of my life.

Thanks also to Patricia Maxwell, another very supportive friend, who offered helpful suggestions and complimentary remarks that I greatly appreciated because she is a real artist.

Lell Forehand typed the first copy many years ago and believed in my story even then. I value her friendship.

To Fred Smith, who has helped me so many times, again shared his expertise in the reproduction of the illustrations. Fred has expertise in many areas; I am fortunate to have such a friend.

(My expertise is in picking friends...good and helpful ones.)

Many thanks to Drake, who nightly critiqued my added thoughts and illustrations. He was helpful and kind to his mother!

Being so taken with Bill and Bo's kind remarks after their first reading and offering to publish, I began a path of discovery with them. I was excited to meet each week for their help and their astute observations and suggestions. But their main help was in the excitement and interest they showed in my story and illustrations each time we met. Our sessions, over coffee at the Two Story Coffee House, became discussions of many subjects and were interesting and fun. We were certainly on the same wave-length in many areas, and they became my editors, publishers and friends.

I must acknowledge the presence of Johnny in all of my undertakings with this book. He always encouraged me, listening to all my writings and reminiscing with me. Because of our love for each other, we were able to come through the times in stories that are not in this book. He would be so proud.

The real T. Tiny and E. Toad A' Thomas

CPSIA information can be obtained
at www.ICGtesting.com
Printed in the USA
LVIC042205140213
320213LV00008B